The I'M NOT SCARED Book

TODD PARR

Megan Tingley Books

LITTLE, BROWN AND COMPANY

New York   Boston

Sometimes I'm scared of the dark.

I'm not scared if I have a night-light.

Sometimes I'm scared of dogs.

I'm not scared when they give me kisses.

Sometimes I'm scared to ride on an airplane.

Sometimes I'm scared of monsters and ghosts.

I'm not scared when I see that
they aren't real.

Sometimes I'm scared of what's under my bed.

I'm not scared once I clean everything out and see all my favorite toys.

Sometimes I'm scared when my family argues.

I'm not scared when we hug and say I'm sorry.

Sometimes I'm scared to go shopping for new underwear.

I'm not scared when I wear them on my head.

Sometimes I'm scared I will get lost in the grocery store.

I'm not scared when I stay close to Mommy.

Sometimes I'm scared on my first day of school.

I'm not scared when I make new friends.

Sometimes I'm scared of thunder and lightning.

I'm not scared when I build a fort
with my best friend.

Sometimes I'm scared when I do something wrong.

I'm not scared when I help to fix it.

Sometimes I'm scared I will make a mistake.

...n not scared when I know I tried my best.

Sometimes I'm scared I'm not perfect.

I'm not scared when I meet someone just like me.

Sometimes we are scared of things  because we don't understand them. When you are afraid, tell someone why and maybe you won't be scared anymore.

THE END. LEV, Todd